Rolf Lidberg
Text: Jan Lööf

Trolls

Translated by Kari Engen

Carlsen FORLAG

One day in March, father troll went to sleep in a heap of snow.

"I've had enough," he said to himself, wrapped an old blanket around him and crawled beneath the snow.

Father troll was waiting for spring! He had been peering into the sky to see if he could catch a glimpse of the spring sun, but it never came.

Everything was so dark and gloomy that he could just as well go to sleep. He didn't know how long he slept, but when he awoke the snow had almost disappeared.

And there was Sarah and her little brother standing next to him. They had picked bunches of coltsfoot and blue anemone. Father troll suddenly realized what had happened.

Spring had come at last!

In raw and cold weather father troll's old joints creaked and groaned. But now that spring had come, he felt young again. He couldn't resist the temptation to run down the hill towards the village where the troll children were playing hop scotch.

"Make room! Here I come! I want to play as well!" father troll shouted.

All the children giggled, he looked really funny! He had some trouble balancing when he tried hopping on one leg. Farther down the road two old troll women were watching and laughing. They were wondering what on earth had happened to father troll. He didn't normally behave like that!

The days passed quickly now that the spring had come. The trolls didn't have to wait long before the summer was at hand. The weather was warm and the sun was shining.

One troll family was sitting by the waterfront. The smallest girl sat on her mother's lap, watching Sarah play in the sand with the toy cows that father troll hade made out of cones.

"To think that the summer is here again," mother troll said.

"It's nice," father troll said. "After having to stay inside a tiny cabin the entire winter, we need to be out in the open air."

Deep in the forest everything was dark and quiet and no birds were singing. Humans didn't like the troll forest. They were afraid they would get lost and never find their way out again.

The trolls however, didn't feel that way. It was their forest and they knew every bit of it. They padded about, gathering cones and looking for mushrooms.

Sarah liked to be in the troll forest. She liked to walk around barefoot in the soft moss and play by herself. One day in June, Sarah discovered something very strange. There were flowers in the midst of the trees. Beautiful, pink flowers!

"I have to tell old grandpa," she thought and hurried home.

"Humans have a strange name for this flower, calypso bulbosaor something like that," grandpa explained. "But we trolls call it the winterflower. When they appear, the winter will be a long and cold one."

"A real troll winter!" old grandpa predicted. "Cold and dark with lots and lots of snow."

"Why can't it be summer for ever?" Sarah asked. "I don't like winter."

"Don't you worry," mother troll said. "Just look at me, I've been through a lot of troll winters and managed well. But one has to prepare oneself thoroughly."

And so mother troll took the children with her out to the marsh to pick cotton grass. The smallest girl fell asleep while Sarah and her little brother helped mother troll fill the bags one by one with the finest white cotton. Then mother troll spun woolthread which she weaved into cloth. And she used the cloth to make warm troll clothes for the winter.

Now all the trolls knew what to expect. But warm clothes alone weren't enough. To survive a troll winter you need a lot of food as well. And by the time the salmon started to move upstream into the rivers, the fishing nets were brought out. A lot of the nets were torn and useless, so the old troll men and women helped each other make new ones.

The trolls were lucky, there were a lot of fish that year. When they hauled in their nets, they were full of flopping salmons. The salmon was roasted over the fire and the trolls ate as much as they wanted. When they had finished the rest of the catch had to be cleaned. Some of the fish was smoked and some of it was pickled, but most of it was hung to dry. Dried fish will keep the best during an entire winter.

Sarah's little brother's name was Morten. He was too young to haul a fishing net.

"I want to fish as well!" Morten cried, but the grown-ups merely pushed him away. In the afternoon uncle Evan discovered Morten-Morten sitting on a rock, all alone and with a sulky look on his face.

"Cheer up!" uncle Evan said. "Why don't you and I go up to the tarn and see if we can catch some trout!"

That made Morten happy again. By the evening he had caught a big trout all by himself and was very proud.

Uncle Evan made up a fire and suggested that they fry the trout for supper. But Morten didn't answer. He was tired after the long day and had fallen asleep, still clutching the fish in his arms. Uncle Evan chuckled and gently spread his jacket over little Morten.

The summer passed quickly. As autumn approached the days grew shorter. There were plenty of berries and mushroom in the woods and the trolls gathered everything that could be eaten.

Morten was good at picking berries. So he thought. And so he was. At least compared to Mary, his little sister. She ate all the berries she picked and in addition she knocked over one of grandmother's punnets.

But it didn't really matter, because the trolls picked such a great quantity of berries that the old troll women were busy making syrup and jam for a whole week. It was all put into the cellars together with the potatoes and the turnips. And in the woodsheds they had stacked piles of dried fish. Now they would manage.

One day uncle Evan and little Morten went for a walk in the forest.

"What happens to all the animals in the forest when it gets cold?" Morten asked.

Uncle Evan told him. About the roe-deers and the hares and all the other animals getting a thick winter fur to withstand the cold, about the squirrel and about the hedgehog that slept in a nest under the ground. And about the birds. Quite a few birds can make it through the winter so they stay, but some move to warmer countries.

"Why don't trolls move to a warmer place in the winter?" Morten asked.

"Trolls can't fly and it's too far to walk," uncle Evan answered. "Besides, trolls manage just fine."

Morten kept on walking along the path, thinking about what uncle Evan had told him. Suddenly the forest ended.

"Look over there, at the bog," Uncle Evan whispered. "The elves are dancing."

"Elves! Where do they go in the winter?" Morten asked.

"Well, they just disappear. I don't know where to. One can't know everything," uncle Evan answered.

The Great Lake was as smooth as a mirror. The air was bright, but a bit cool. The troll family had been out rowing on the lake and were about to go ashore. On beautiful summer evenings they often brought their sandwiches with them in the boat and had their evening meal while watching the sunset. Today however, they could feel that autumn had come.

"This is the last time this year!" father troll said. "Now we have to take the boat ashore and scrape and clean it before winter."

"But it isn't winter yet," Morten said.

"Your father knows what he's doing," mother troll said. "The cold weather can be here any day now. Just take a look at the mountain-tops over there."

There Morten disovered the first white patches of snow.

The first snow came one day at the end of October. But when the sun peered through the clouds, the snow soon disappeared again. The troll children were playing with marbles on the road.

"What do you mean by walking around barefoot this time of year?" grandpa troll said.

"We're not a bit cold," the boys replied.

They were so excited and taken up by their game, they hadn't noticed how cold it had become.

"Well, well," grandpa said. "I was just like that when I was a boy, too."

But the next day, the boys had put on both socks and shoes before they went out to play. Suddenly it had become really cold!

The weather became so cold that the lake froze and the next day the ice was thick enough to walk upon. All the troll children got out their skates and ran down to the lake.

Sarah had learnt how to skate last winter, although she had forgotten most of it during the summer. She tried a few cautious uncertain steps and she didn't do too badly. As soon as she tried to turn however, she lost her balance and fell down on her bottom.

A boy troll named Truls helped her up on her feet again. Truls was very good at skating, he took Sarah's hand and suddenly it wasn't at all difficult any longer.

Truls and Sarah skated together all evening, continuing even after it had become dark and the moon had risen.

By the time it had been snowing for several weeks the children could no longer skate on The Great Lake. Instead, they went skiing or used their sledges.

But father troll often sat out on the lake, all by himself. He had made a little hole in the ice and he could sit there for hours, fishing. He hardly ever caugth anything and when he did, it was usually a miserable little perch.

Once in a while mother troll and little Wiggo went out to visit him. Mother troll brought him coffee and sandwiches.

"You've only caught one little fish today," Wiggo said, cautiously poking at the perch. "So why do you sit here?"

"Who knows," father troll said and scratched his beard.

"I think I know why," mother troll said. "It's not because of the fish. It's because father troll likes to sit here alone and ponder over life and all sorts of things."

"Mother is probably right, she always is," the old man said and smiled.

The next day it had stopped snowing. "I'm tired of fishing," father troll said. "It's time we did something useful."

So he made some sandwiches, then went out into the wood-shed, got out a saw and an axe and put everything on the sleigh.

"You're going with me to the woods, as well, Morten!" father troll exclaimed. "You have grown big and strong this summer and now you have to take your part working in the forest."

Morten felt very proud, normally only the grown up trolls were allowed to come along.

Father troll and Morten started cutting down the trees. You need a lot of wood to keep the troll cabins warm during a long winter. The forest crashed and creaked as the big trees fell, scaring off the birds in all directions.

But when father troll and Morten sat down to eat their sandwiches, the birds returned. A little tit, not being at all afraid, landed on father troll's sandwich and started pecking at it.

One evening at the end of December, Sarah's grandmother held a party for all the troll children. Grandmother had made ricepudding and because grandfather loved ricepudding, he was invited as well.

"I have learnt this from the humans," grandmother said." They always eat ricepudding on this particular evening."

"I have heard that the children get presents as well," Sarah said, "presents with nice things in them."

"We want presents, too!" all the troll children shouted.

"Now really!" grandmother said. "You get presents for your birthday and that ought to be enough."

"Personally, I think it's a good idea," grandfather said. He loved presents.

"Is that so? Maybe I have to think about it then," grandmother said and stirred the porridge.

Before the children went to bed, Sarah and Wiggo went for a walk to the top of the hill. Wiggo was Sarah's youngest brother. He was a bit afraid of the dark and held her hand tightly.

"I just want to show you the stars," Sarah said and pointed towards the starry sky.

Little Wiggo blinked and peered. He had never been outdoors that late before and he had never seen so many stars.

"What a lot of stars," little Wiggo said.

"Yes, that's what the sky looks like on a real winter's night," Sarah said, feeling very solemn.

Sarah thought about the year that had passed. She thought about the summer and the day she had discovered the flowers in the forest. The winter turned out to be long and cold, just like old grandpa had foreseen. But it didn't really matter, Sarah thought. She knew that even a troll winter comes to an end and then the spring would come again.